The Rose Island Lighthouse Series

THE CURIOUS CHILDHOOD OF WANTON CHASE

Lynne Heinzmann
Julia Heinzmann
Michaela Fournier
Marilyn Harris

NORWALK, CONNECTICUT

Library of Congress Cataloguing-in-Publication Data available

Hardcover - 978-1-949116-06-9
Paperback - 978-1-949116-11-3

First Edition

TABLE OF CONTENTS

IMAGE AND ILLUSTRATION CREDITS

The following individuals and organizations have generously given permission to reprint images in this book.

Front Cover: Leaving Rose Island – Original artwork by Julia T. Heinzmann; Graphic design by Michaela M. Fournier.
Page 7: Wanton at the Lighthouse – Original artwork by Julia T. Heinzmann.
Pages 8 to 9: Fog Signal Building and Bell Tower – Collection of National Archives (https://www.archives.gov/research/alic/reference/photography/catalog/rose_island_lighthouse/1907409321); 6th Order Fresnel Lens – Collection of Rose Island Lighthouse Foundation; Lighthouse Service Oil Lamp – Courtesy of Kenrich A. Claflin & Sons Nautical Antiques (www.lighthouseantiques.net); SS Narragansett (ship), 1908 – Collection of Rose Island Lighthouse Foundation; Rose Island Lighthouse – Collection of Rose Island Lighthouse Foundation.
Page 10: Grandfather and Wanton – Original artwork by Julia T. Heinzmann.
Pages 12 to 13: U.S. Lighthouse Service Pennant – Courtesy of Kenrich A. Claflin & Sons Nautical Antiques (www.lighthouseantiques.net); Captain Charles Curtis – Collection of Rose Island Lighthouse Foundation.
Page 15: Wanton Snitching Cookies – Original artwork by Julia T. Heinzmann.
Pages 16 to 17: Recipe Cards – Original artwork by Michaela M. Fournier; Mixing Bowl, Spoon, and Cookies – Original artwork by Julia T. Heinzmann.
Page 18: Doctor Stephens – Original artwork by Julia T. Heinzmann.
Pages 20 to 21: All images Collection of National Library of Medicine: Mrs. Winslow's Soothing Syrup – (http://resource.nlm.nih.gov/101402395); Clark Stanley's Snake Oil Liniment, From True Life in the Far West, 200 page pamphlet, illus., Worcester, Massachusetts, c. 1905 – (https://www.nlm.nih.gov/exhibition/ephemera/medshow.html); Household Manual of Medicine – (https://collections.nlm.nih.gov/catalog/nlm:nlmuid-63580140R-bk); Doctor's Black Bag – (https://www.ncbi.nlm.nih.gov/pmc/articles/PMC3255184/).
Page 23: Wanton Digging a Fort – Original artwork by Julia T. Heinzmann.
Pages 24 to 25: Historic Site Plan – Collection of United States Library of Congress (https://www.loc.gov.pictures/item/ri0477.sheet0003a); Aerial View During WWII – Collection of Rose Island Lighthouse Foundation; Officer's Housing – Collection of Rose Island Lighthouse Foundation.
Page 26: Norman and Wanton Searching for Treasure – Original artwork by Julia T. Heinzmann.
Pages 28 to 29: Lewis Sargent (actor) Playing Marbles – Exhibitor's Herald, December 4, 1920, p. 50 (https://archive.org/details/exhibitorsherald11exhi_1/page/n7); Patent for Liquid Pistol – Collection of United State Patent Office (https://search.uspto.gov/item/600.552/); Baseball Glove circa 1904 – Courtesy of United States Library of Congress (http://chroniclingamerica.loc.gov/lccn/sn88085187/1904-04-28/ed1/seq-3/ (The Tacoma Times); Original "Teddy's Bear" Cartoon – By Clifford Berryman, published in Washington Post, 1902 (public domain), via Wikimedia Commons (https://commons.wikimedia.org/wiki/File:TheodoreRooseveltTeddyBear.jpg).
Page 31: The Outhouse – Original artwork by Julia T. Heinzmann.
Pages 32 to 33: President Woodrow Wilson – By Harris & Ewing (public domain), via Wikimedia Commons (https://commons.wikimedia.org/wiki/File:Thomas_Woodrow_Wilson,_Harris_%26_Ewing_bw_photo_portrait,_1919.jpg); Typical Home 1915 – By Internet Archive Book Images (no restrictions), via Wikimedia Commons (https://commons.wikimedia.org/wiki/File:A_plan_book_of_Harris_homes_(1915)_(14598191658).jpg); The Birth of A Nation (Movie Poster) – By Unknown Author (public domain), via Wikimedia Commons (https://commons.wikimedia.org/wiki/File:Birth_of_a_Nation_poster_2.jpg).
Pages 34 to 35: Wanton in Newport – Original artwork by Julia T. Heinzmann.
Pages 36 to 37: U.S. Naval Station Newport in the 1900s – By U.S. Department of Defense (U.S. Navy All Hands magazine July 1964, p. 61.) (public domain), via Wikimedia Commons (https://commons.wikimedia.org/wiki/File:Naval_Station_Newport_RI_in_the_1900s.jpg); Belview Avenue, Newport, RI, Postcard – By the Metropolitan News Co., Boston, MA, From the Collection of Lynne M. Heinzmann; The Breakers (Mansion) – By Unknow Author (public domain), via Wikimedia Commons (https://commons.wikimedia.org/wiki/File:Breakers_(1878)_-_Newport,_RI.jpg).
Page 39: Wanton and Dixie – Original artwork by Julia T. Heinzmann.
Pages 40 to 41: Roger's High School, Newport, RI, Postcard – By Unknow Author (public domain), via Wikimedia Commons (https://commons.wikimedia.org/wiki/File:Rogers_High_School_(1907)_-_Newport,_RI.jpg); 1915 Rules for Teachers – Information by Unknown Author (public domain), via Open Culture (www.openculture.com), Graphics by Lynne M. Heinzmann.
Page 42: Leaving Rose Island – Original artwork by Julia T. Heinzmann.
Pages 44 to 45: HMS Lusitania – By George Grantham Bain (public domain), via Wikimedia Commons (https://commons.wikimedia.org/wiki/File:RMS_Lusitania_coming_into_port,_possibly_in_New_York,_1907-13-crop.jpg); German Submarine U-53 in Newport Harbor, November 1916 – By Bain (Library of Congress) (public domain), via Wikimedia Commons (https://commons.wikimedia.org/wiki/File:SM_U-53_in_Newport,_Rhode_Island_1916.jpg); WWI Recruitment Poster – By James Montgomery Flagg (public domain), via Wikimedia Commons (https://commons.wikimedia.org/wiki/File:Uncle_sam_propaganda_in_ww1.jpg).
Pages 46 to 47: Restoration of Rose Island Lighthouse and Rose Island Lighthouse Foundation Logo – Collection of Rose Island Lighthouse Foundation; 1984 Lighthouse – By Curt Bunting; 2012 Lighthouse – By Charlotte E. Johnson.
Rear Cover: Recollections of Life on Rose Island – By Wanton Chase, via Collection of Rose Island Lighthouse Foundation; Graphic design by Michaela M. Fournier.

INTRODUCTION

During America's Revolutionary War, the British built a fort on Rose Island, an 18-acre parcel of marsh grass located in Narragansett Bay, halfway between Jamestown and Newport, Rhode Island. After the war, the U.S. Government renamed the installation Fort Hamilton and made several additions to it, including two circular tower bastions, a citadel, and a large barracks building. In 1869, just after the American Civil War, a lighthouse was built atop one of the fort's bastions to guide boats through the rocky bay. Originally operated by the U.S. Lighthouse Service, the Coast Guard was given control of the lighthouse in 1941 and managed it until 1971, when the light was decommissioned.

A young boy named Wanton Chase lived in the Rose Island Lighthouse from 1910 to 1916, from the time he was 1 to 7 years old. His grandfather, Charles Curtis, was lighthouse keeper there (1887 to 1918), while his grandmother, Christina McPhee Curtis, took care of the cooking and all their other domestic needs.

Wanton's life on Rose Island was fairly solitary. When weather permitted, his mother, brother, and sisters visited him on weekends and occasionally he made friends with the children of officers stationed at Fort Hamilton, but most of the time Wanton played alone, wandering the island's beaches to see what the tide had washed ashore.

Later in life, Wanton Chase recorded his memories of his adventures on Rose Island. His written recollections are the basis for the story chapters of this book. The history chapters contain additional factual information and photographs to provide context for the stories. We hope you enjoy getting to know Wanton and Rose Island.

WANTON ARRIVES AT THE LIGHTHOUSE

Mabel Chase sat on the bench and leaned back against the lighthouse wall. Smiling, she watched her three children chase an orange butterfly as it flitted from one golden dandelion to the next in the warm August sunshine. Her smile faded as she noticed only Norman and Christina were running after the butterfly. Wanton, her youngest, sat on a blanket in the middle of the lighthouse lawn, watching his siblings and gasping for breath. He had been a sickly boy since he was born eighteen months ago, always pale and coughing and often running a fever. To tell the truth, Mabel was surprised he'd lived this long. Her constant worrying about him wore her out.

Mabel's mother, Christina McPhee Curtis, clomped down the kitchen steps and handed her a bowl of green beans she'd picked from the lighthouse garden that morning. Plopping an empty bowl between them, her mom sat heavily on the bench and cracked the ends off one of the beans. Nodding toward Wanton, she said, "It's time, Mabel."

"Time for what?"

"Time to leave Wanton here with Father and me." She gently touched Mabel's arm. "Look, I know you love the boy—he sure is a sweet child—but if you want him to have any chance of growing up, he needs to be outdoors in the sea air."

Mabel pointed a green bean toward the lawn. "He is outdoors, Mother. Every weekend the weather is agreeable we come out to visit."

Her mother shook her head. "He needs to be outdoors all the time."

They'd had this same conversation dozens of times. Deep down, Mabel knew her mother was right. But the idea of leaving her baby here on Rose Island and only seeing him on weekends made her feel sad. Despite his ill-health, Wanton was a happy child who brought her joy. She snapped another bean and gazed across Newport Harbor toward Jamestown. A line of white sailboats darted back and forth in the gray-blue water, racing each other to the top mark buoy near Goat Island, just to swing around it and try to beat each other back to the start line. She remembered many times when she and her brother Samuel were younger and lived in the lighthouse, they would row the skiff out toward the buoy, trying to go faster than the racing sailboats. She wondered if Wanton would ever be healthy enough to do something like that with his brother or sister. And who would play with him during the week? Her mother and father were too busy with their lighthouse duties to pay much attention to Wanton. Of course, there might be children living in the fort's officers' housing. Or there might not.

Mabel's mother patted her knee and picked up the bean bowls. "It's time," she repeated as she tromped up the stairs to begin cooking dinner.

Mabel dropped her hands into the lap of her red-and-white checkered dress and studied her youngest son. Even from this distance, she could see his tiny shoulders rise and fall as he struggled to pull air into his lungs. His blond curls floated in the sea breezes as he smiled at his brother and sister. But Wanton hardly moved his arms or legs, as if his smiling took all the energy he had.

And, just like that, Mabel made her decision: she'd leave her son here with her parents. Today. She had to. Like her mother said, it was the only chance Wanton had to survive. When she returned home to Newport that night, she'd explain things to her husband, Stephen. He'd understand because he worried about Wanton, too.

Mabel stood. "Watch out for your little brother," she called out to six-year-old Norman and four-year-old Christina. Then she turned and climbed the stairs to help her mother prepare dinner.

THE ROSE ISLAND LIGHTHOUSE

In 1868, just after the Civil War, the United States Congress approved $7,500 for the construction of a lighthouse on Rose Island to help guide boats through the mouth of Narragansett Bay. The island, an 18-acre spit of marsh grass located a mile offshore of Newport, Rhode Island, was already home to Fort Hamilton, a barracks and munitions storage facility and part of the nation's coastal defense system. Constructed of wood, the one-and-a-half story, mansard-roofed lighthouse was nearly identical to three others in the area, all designed by Vermont architect, Albert Dow. Rose Island's 8-sided tower housed a 6th order beehive-shaped Fresnel lens that shot a beam of red light 48 feet above the water.

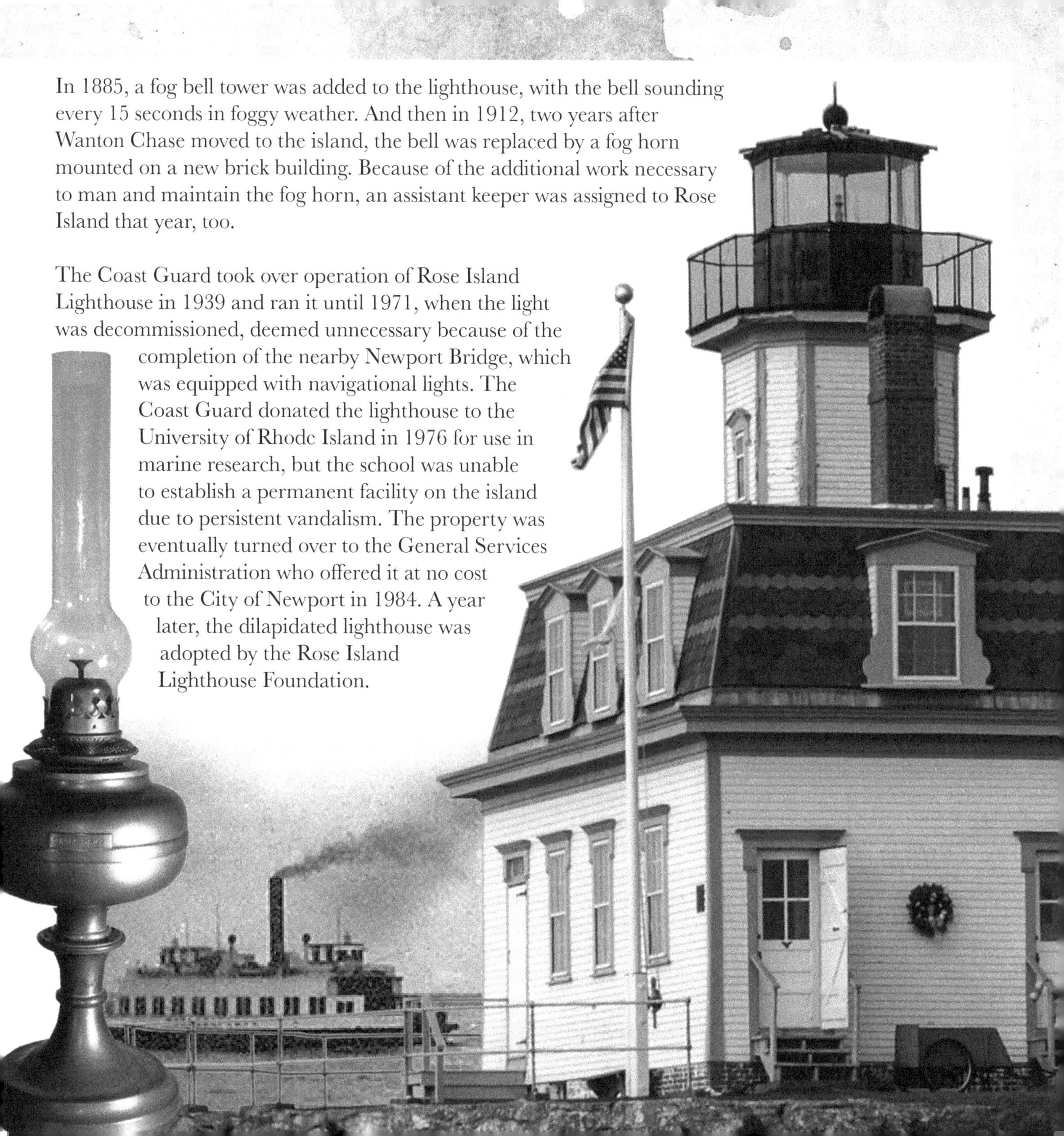

In 1885, a fog bell tower was added to the lighthouse, with the bell sounding every 15 seconds in foggy weather. And then in 1912, two years after Wanton Chase moved to the island, the bell was replaced by a fog horn mounted on a new brick building. Because of the additional work necessary to man and maintain the fog horn, an assistant keeper was assigned to Rose Island that year, too.

The Coast Guard took over operation of Rose Island Lighthouse in 1939 and ran it until 1971, when the light was decommissioned, deemed unnecessary because of the completion of the nearby Newport Bridge, which was equipped with navigational lights. The Coast Guard donated the lighthouse to the University of Rhode Island in 1976 for use in marine research, but the school was unable to establish a permanent facility on the island due to persistent vandalism. The property was eventually turned over to the General Services Administration who offered it at no cost to the City of Newport in 1984. A year later, the dilapidated lighthouse was adopted by the Rose Island Lighthouse Foundation.

ASSISTANT KEEPER

Just after sunrise, three-year-old Wanton shuffled into the lighthouse's kitchen, still wearing his cotton nightshirt and wool socks, and rubbing the sleep from his blue-green eyes. He found Grandfather eating his oatmeal at the kitchen table, with Grandmother standing across the room, watching the coffee bubble up into the glass knob of the coffee pot. Grandfather had just extinguished the lighthouse lantern for the day and was eating his breakfast before going back up to the tower to clean and polish the Fresnel lens that magnified and focused the lantern's beam. Wanton tried to get up at this time every morning so he could help Grandfather polish the beautiful beehive-shaped lens, passing him the cleaner and rags when he asked for them.

Grandfather saw Wanton and nodded toward an empty chair. "Take a seat, son." Looking over his shoulder, he said, "Mother, get him some breakfast."

By the time Wanton climbed up to the table, a steaming bowl of oatmeal sat in front of him, fixed just the way he liked it—swimming in maple syrup.

Pointing his spoon toward the window, Grandfather asked, "Son, do you see those pink clouds?" The sun was just poking up over the city of Newport, giving the white church steeples a rosy glow.

Wanton nodded, his mouth full of sweet oatmeal.

"Know what they mean?"

Wanton shook his head and took another bite.

"'Red sky at night, sailors' delight. Red sky in morning, sailors take warning.' Ever hear that before?"

"No sir," Wanton said, licking his sticky lips.

"It means we're in for some rough weather today. This afternoon… or this evening, at the latest."

Wanton frowned. "But the sky's pink, not red."

Grandmother handed them each a metal cup of coffee, and then added a large amount of milk to Wanton's cup, turning the liquid from dark brown to light tan.

Grandfather chuckled. "Pink…red…it doesn't matter. With the way the barometer's falling, we're in for a whale of a Nor'easter."

Wanton's eyes opened wide with worry. He knew a Nor'easter was a bad kind of storm. One had blown ashore last month with enough power to damage the landing and crack one of the huge windows in the lantern room.

Grandfather clapped a hand on Wanton's thin shoulder. "We'll be fine, son. But I'll need some extra help from you."

Wanton looked up at his grandfather's lined face and bushy moustache. "From me?"

Grandfather nodded. "Mr. Fletcher is visiting his family in town, so you're going to have to be my assistant keeper for the day. Do you think you can do that?"

Wanton nodded solemnly.

Grandfather patted Wanton's blond head. "I knew I could count on you." He picked up his grandson, who was very small for his age, and placed him on the wooden floor. "Now, hurry up and get dressed. Warm clothes. It's cold out there already and getting colder by the minute."

"Yes, sir." Wanton ran around the corner, heading toward his bedroom.

DUTIES OF THE ROSE ISLAND LIGHTHOUSE KEEPER

In the early 20th Century, the profession of lighthouse keeper was considered one of the most difficult jobs to have. The keeper and his/her family usually lived at the lighthouse and worked 24 hours a day, 7 days a week, in very isolated and difficult conditions. When blizzards, gales, hurricanes, or other foul weather occurred, the keeper worked even harder to keep the lamp burning and to assist imperiled mariners. He/she was also expected to perform all of the repair and maintenance required for the entire lighthouse station.

In 1886, Wanton's grandfather, Captain Charles Curtis, became the fifth consecutive keeper of the Rose Island Lighthouse after having been a Union officer in the Civil War, a policeman in Newport, RI, and the keeper of the Light at Sakonnet Point off the coast of Little Compton, RI. Together with his wife, Christina (McPhee), and their family, Captain Curtis served at Rose Island for 31 years, longer than any other keeper. During his time there, he witnessed significant changes to the lighthouse: a fog horn tower was added on the rocks below the west end and the second story of the lighthouse was renovated to create an apartment for an assistant keeper. His assistant, Julius Johanssen and then Charles Fletcher, was responsible for the maintenance and use of the new fog horn, but Captain Curtis supervised its operation and the operation of all other aspects of the lighthouse.

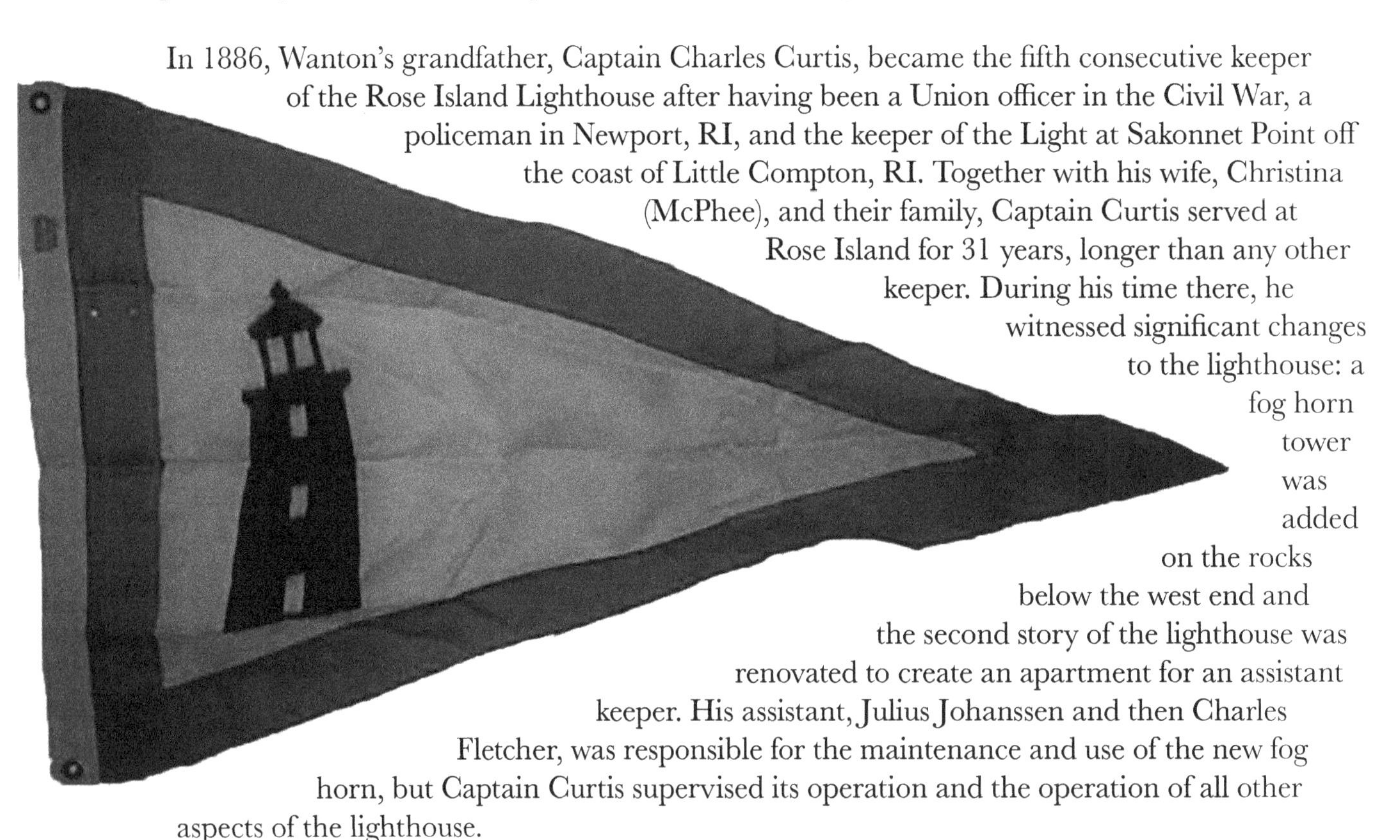

This is a list of Captain Curtis's duties as the Rose Island Lighthouse Keeper, which was fairly typical for most New England keepers of that era:

- Oversee the sounding of the fog horn every 15 seconds when heavy fog is present (day or night)
- Fill the beacon lamp with kerosene and trim the wicks daily
- Light the beacon lamp at sunset (after the sundown gun sounds from Newport's Fort Adams) and keep it burning all night, every night
- Clean and polish the Fresnel lens daily
- Clean and polish the lantern room windows daily
- Clean, repair, and paint all lighthouse station buildings
- Maintain all station grounds and walkways
- Record all lighthouse station activities in a log book daily
- Take and record all weather readings in a log book daily
- Maintain an accurate inventory of all lighthouse station supplies
- Take depth soundings of bay and move channel markers
- Provide assistance to mariners in distress
- Ensure lighthouse station boats (skiff and launch) are in good working order at all times
- Clean lighthouse station outhouse regularly and apply lime
- Provide lighthouse station tours when requested
- Maintain a clean uniform at all times
- Plant and maintain a personal garden annually

Captain Charles Curtis (Wanton's Grandfather)

SNITCHING COOKIES

Three-and-a-half-year-old Wanton knew Grandfather was napping on his bed in the living room. He napped every afternoon, so he could stay up all night to tend the light and oversee the sounding of the fog horn when it was foggy. But Wanton wasn't tiptoeing into the kitchen to avoid waking Grandfather. He was trying to snitch a sugar cookie from the sweets drawer even though Grandmother was standing right there at the stove, frying fish cakes for dinner. Wanton silently placed his soggy cloth bag on the chair next to the door. Holding his breath, he grabbed the shiny handle with both hands and quietly slid the drawer open. One inch. Two inches. Three. Four. The sweet, buttery smell of cookies filled his nose and made his mouth water. Slowly, he reached into the drawer…and felt a sharp tap on his shoulder. His hands fell to his sides as he sighed loudly. He turned and looked up at an unsmiling face, wreathed by fuzzy white hair.

"Sorry, Grandmother," he mumbled.

She frowned and whispered, "You know better than to eat cookies right before dinner."

Wanton looked down at his sandy feet and wondered what his punishment would be this time. Last time, he'd had to sweep the outhouse and then wash its bench and toilet seats while Grandmother stood over him with her hands on her hips. She didn't know that the outhouse scared him. Even the thought of it now made him shiver.

Grandmother nodded at the chair. "Is that my sea moss?"

Wanton picked up the drippy bag and offered it to her with a smile, hoping she'd be so happy to get her seaweed, she'd forget about punishing him. "Are you going to make Vanmonge pudding?" he asked eagerly.

She laughed and carried the bag to the pantry sink, the only sink in the house. "It's called 'Blancmange' pudding…and why should I make it for you, Mr. Cookie Snitcher?" She dumped the seaweed into a big metal colander.

"But I didn't eat any cookies."

"Not for lack of trying." Grandmother wiped her hands on her white apron. "Tell you what. You rinse the sea moss for ten minutes straight and I'll forget about you trying to steal my cookies AND I'll make you your favorite pudding. Do we have a deal?"

Wanton smiled broadly and nodded.

"All right then, young man, climb up here and get to work."

He clambered up on the step stool, grasped the red metal pump handle, and started pumping the water up to the sink from the cistern in the basement. After a few seconds, water poured out of the spigot and splashed on the sandy seaweed.

"Good," Grandmother said. "Now keep that up for ten minutes." She walked back to the stove.

Wanton knew that he'd be tired after manning the pump for that long. But he also knew he liked washing seaweed a whole lot better than cleaning the outhouse.

GRANDMOTHER'S RECIPES

Years later, when Wanton Chase wrote down his memories of his time in the lighthouse, he made several references to the delicious meals that his grandmother prepared and even included some of her recipes in his notes. Here are a few of those recipes:

Blancmange Pudding

1 cup fresh sea moss seaweed
3 cups milk
1/3 cup sugar
1/8 tsp. salt
1 tsp. vanilla

Wash the seaweed in fresh water. Put in a cheesecloth sack and add with milk to top of a double boiler. Cook over boiling water for 25 minutes. Remove the seaweed sack and add sugar, salt, and vanilla to double boiler. Stir until cool and then pour into individual pudding bowls. Chill and serve with berries. Makes 6 half-cup servings.

Sweets Drawer Sugar Cookies

- 1 cup butter, softened
- 2 cups sugar
- 2 eggs
- 2 tablespoons milk
- 1 tsp. vanilla
- 3 cups flour
- 2 tsp. baking powder
- ½ tsp. salt

Cream butter and sugar. Add eggs, milk, and vanilla. Mix thoroughly. Sift together flour, baking powder, and salt and add gradually to creamed mixture. Mix thoroughly. Cover and chill 6 hours, minimum. Shape dough into ¾ inch balls. Place 2" apart on greased baking sheet. Flatten with bottom of a glass that has been greased and dipped in sugar. Bake at 375 degrees for 8 to 10 minutes or until edges are golden brown. Cool on rack. Makes about 3 dozen cookies.

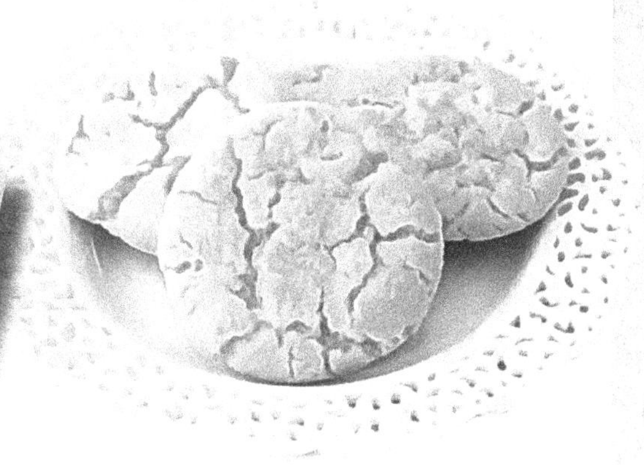

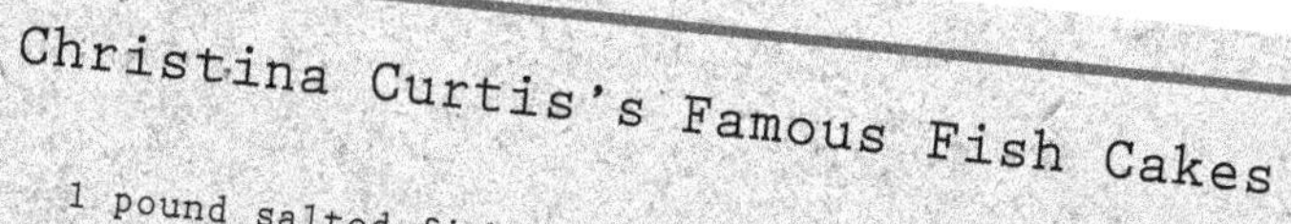

Christina Curtis's Famous Fish Cakes

- 1 pound salted fish
- 4 medium white potatoes
- 1 medium onion
- 2 eggs
- Salt and pepper to taste

Boil fish until tender and flaky, then crumble in medium bowl and allow to cool. Boil potatoes and mash. Chop onion finely and add to fish. Add all other ingredients; mix thoroughly. Form into 3" cakes and fry in hot oil until golden brown. Serve immediately. Makes 8 fish cakes.

THE DOCTOR

When Grandmother called in nearly-four-year-old Wanton from beachcombing one sunny April morning, he thought she was going to ask him to entertain his little cousins. Uncle Sam and Aunt Bessie were visiting the lighthouse for the day and they seemed to expect Wanton to play with two-year-old Harold and baby Charles. But when Wanton crested the hill and saw Grandmother pacing back and forth near the kitchen door, wringing her white apron with both hands, he knew something was terribly wrong.

Grandmother grasped both of his elbows. "Wanton, quick, run over to the barracks and tell them we need a doctor here, right away. The baby swallowed an open safety pin and now he's coughing terribly and can't catch his breath. If the doctor is not there, ask them to call one in from Newport. Then go down to the pier and wait for him. Bring the doctor up here as soon as he arrives."

Wanton ran at his top speed all the way to the barracks. Forty minutes later when Dr. Stephens stepped from the Navy launch onto the pier, Wanton grabbed his hand and dragged him at a fast trot up the path to the lighthouse, with the doctor's instruments jangling in his black leather bag.

Grandmother met them at the kitchen door and quickly ushered Dr. Stephens into the bedroom while Grandfather led Wanton toward the bench near the bastion's south wall. Grandfather had a red-and-white checked kitchen towel tied around his head, holding an ice bag against his cheek to alleviate a toothache that had been plaguing him for three days, now. He groaned as he sat down with Wanton.

"Is Charles going to get better?" Wanton asked anxiously.

Patting Wanton's knee, Grandfather said, "We'll see, son. The doctor will do all he can for the boy. We'll just have to wait and see what happens." His words sounded garbled, as if he were talking with a mouthful of marbles. The two of them sat in silence, watching seagulls drop oysters on the rocks and then swoop down to pick up the exposed meat.

Around noontime, the kitchen door opened and Dr. Stephens stepped out onto the lawn, slowly sliding his arms into the sleeves of his wrinkled brown jacket. Sounds of weeping could be heard coming from the lighthouse.

Grandfather sighed and then rose to his feet. "So, no good, huh?"

Dr. Stephens shook his head sadly. "Fluid built up around his heart in reaction to the ingested pin and his body just couldn't handle the stress. Wouldn't have mattered if you had taken him to the hospital in Newport; there was nothing that could be done for the lad."

"Did the baby die?" Wanton whispered from the bench.

Grandfather nodded and then patted the doctor's shoulder. "I'm sure you did everything you could, Bob."

The doctor pointed toward Grandfather's jaw. "What about you, Charles? Want me to look at that for you?"

"It's my danged tooth. Been hurting me for days, now."

Opening his bag on the bench, Dr. Stephens said, "Sit down. Let me take a look." After poking around in Grandfather's mouth for a minute, making the big man wince several times, the doctor said, "It's a rotten molar that needs to come out. Come see me at my office sometime next week."

"Can you do it now?" Grandfather asked.

"I don't have any anesthetic with me."

"No matter. Just pull it out. Nothing you do could hurt as much as this is already."

The doctor raised his eyebrows. "If you're sure…?" At Grandfather's nod, he lifted a pair of shiny pliers from his bag. "Brace yourself."

Grandfather put his hand on Wanton's knee and nodded once more.

Dr. Stephens grasped the bad tooth with the pliers, grabbed Grandfather's jaw with the other hand, and pulled hard, his face turning red with his exertion.

After two or three minutes of yanking and twisting—with Grandfather squeezing Wanton's leg harder and harder—the tooth came out with a small pop.

Dr. Stephens inspected the offending tooth. "Surprisingly, it looks like it came out in one piece, so you should be feeling much better soon." He dropped his pliers and the tooth into his bag. "Make sure you rinse your mouth with salt water several times a day and pack that hole with clean cotton rags until it stops bleeding."

Grandfather stood up, spat blood over the wall, and shook the doctor's hand again. "Will do. Thanks, Doc." Turning to Wanton, he said, "We'd best go in to see Uncle Sam and Aunt Bessie. Little Harold, too. They'll all be needing our support, right about now."

Wanton walked slowly with Grandfather back to the lighthouse while Dr. Stephens crunched down the shell-strewn path to the pier to take the launch back to Newport.

MEDICINE IN AMERICA

In 1913, the year that Wanton Chase's young cousin died on Rose Island, American medicine was still in its infancy. Life expectancy at birth was just 49.4 years. Only 13 percent of American babies were born in hospitals – versus being born at home with or without the assistance of a midwife – and one in ten children died before he was twelve months old. Ninety percent of American doctors had no formal education; they had been self-taught or had learned the "medical arts" from older family members or from other un-schooled doctors. Surgeries were performed by doctors as a last resort, at home, in very unsterile conditions. If a wound became infected—a common occurrence—it was essentially untreatable, since neither sulfa drugs nor antibiotics were yet available.

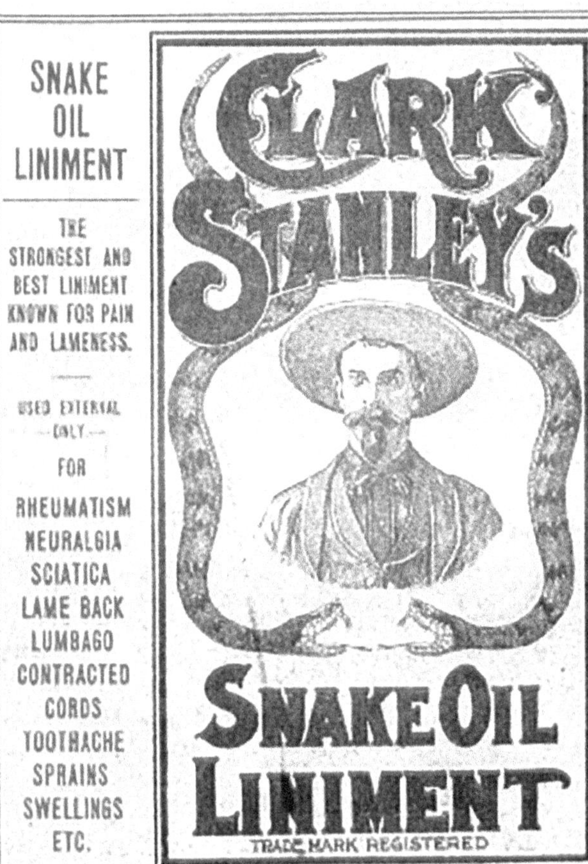

Many Americans obtained their primary medical advice from household medical guides such as "The Practical Family Doctor," which sold for $1.45 in the 1908 Sears, Roebuck & Co. Catalogue. These guides included information about such diverse topics as diseases of women, diseases of children, marriage, pregnancy, and the "delicate and wonderful matters pertaining to the nature and relations of the sexes."

Medicines were typically herbal remedies passed down through families from one generation to the next. But some pack peddlers made money selling quack cure-alls that often were ineffective or contained harmful ingredients. Consider Mrs. Winslow's Soothing Syrup for calming teething babies, which contained morphine. Or the many "snake oil" liniments that claimed to cure a wide variety of ailments; they often contained little or no oil from any snake and had no medicinal effect. It wasn't until after The Great War (World War I) that modern medicine came to the United States, through knowledge gained on the battlefields and in field hospitals.

PLAYING SOLDIER 

Early one evening in mid-September, five-year-old Wanton was using a small garden shovel to dig a hole on the top of a hill, making a fort to defend the island. The Great War was raging in Europe—Wanton had heard Grandfather talking about it with a Marine sentry—and Wanton was afraid some of the "bad guys" would try to capture Rose Island. He flung a shovelful of dirt over his shoulder, looked up, and found himself face-to-face with red-headed Roger O'Connor, son of Gunner O'Connor, who lived in one of the Fort Hamilton houses on the island. Although Roger was only a few years older than Wanton, he was a lot taller and a lot heavier.

"What do you have on?" Roger demanded.

Wanton looked at his outfit: cutoff khaki pants belted with a rope, a woman's blue cotton blouse, and a white sailor's cap that constantly flopped down over his eyes. "Just some stuff I found on the beach." He enjoyed wearing clothes that washed up on shore; it made him feel like a pirate.

Roger frowned and shook his head disapprovingly. "And what are you doing?"

"Building a fort."

Why?"

Wanton shrugged. He was afraid Roger would think him a baby for being afraid of "bad guys."

"Well, you're doing it all wrong," Roger said. "A fort should be down on the beach to protect the island from invaders, not back here on a hill. My dad's a Chief in the Navy, so I know these things."

Wanton nodded, wishing Roger would leave him alone so he could go back to digging.

"I'll show you what I mean. You stay up here and try to defend your fort and I'll sneak up on you and capture it."

Wanton wiped his hands on his short pants. "How can I defend my fort? I don't have a water pistol, or anything."

Roger pointed down. "Use some lumps of dirt. I'll get some, too."

"Throw dirt at each other?" Wanton was pretty sure Grandmother would not approve; she was always saying they should be friends.

"Sure. Why not?" Roger said. "You afraid?"

Wanton shook his head.

"Good. Close your eyes and count to twenty, real slow. You can count to twenty, can't you?"

Wanton bit his lip and nodded.

"Good. Count out loud and then I'll attack."

Wanton reluctantly picked up two fist-sized clumps and closed his eyes. "One, two, three, four…" He considered letting Roger win the battle so he'd go home sooner. "…Seventeen, thirteen, twenty." He scanned the bushes all around his fort, looking for signs of the "bad guy." Down in the cove, he heard loons singing out their mournful cries.

Something hit the ground behind him. He turned just as a large clod of dirt knocked off his over-sized sailor's cap. Wanton reached up to find a bleeding cut on his forehead.

Roger ran up the hill and jumped on the wall of the fort, making an avalanche of dirt rain down into the hole. "I hereby conquer this territory in the name of the United States Navy!"

The sundown gun from Newport's Fort Adams boomed across the bay.

Roger stomped his foot, causing another avalanche. "Dang. I have to go home, now. Otherwise, I would have tied you up and made you my prisoner. Lucky for you." He raced down the path and out of sight.

Wanton put on his sailor's cap and pushed it against his wound to make the bleeding stop. Crouching down, he stabbed the shovel into the dirt over and over, thinking about how to beat Roger next time.

Approaching footsteps crunched on the path.

Wanton leapt to his feet and pointed the shovel like a gun. "Hands up!"

A startled Marine sentry aimed his rifle at Wanton and shouted, "Drop your weapon! Immediately!"

Wanton's shovel fell to the ground.

"What the heck?" the sentry said, peering through the failing daylight. "Wanton?"

Wanton nodded, huge tears spilling from his little-boy eyes.

Lowering his rifle, the sentry said, "You should know better than to surprise me like that! I could have killed you! Don't you know there's a war going on?"

By now, Wanton was sobbing uncontrollably.

The Marine put his hand on the boy's shoulder. "Come on, son. I'll walk you home."

FORT HAMILTON

Rose Island was the site of a military installation long before it became home to the lighthouse. The British built a fort on the island during the Revolutionary War, using it as a battery to house artillery (cannons) and soldiers. In 1780 when the French became American allies in the war, their fleet arrived in Newport and the British fled. In 1798, the U.S. Government hired French engineers to help design New England coastal defenses, including additions to the fort on Rose Island.

Renamed Fort Hamilton in honor of Alexander Hamilton, the fort had several different structures, including two circular tower bastions, a citadel, and a supposedly bombproof barracks. Although the fort was never completed, it was constantly occupied. In 1820, it was used as a quarantine hospital for housing cholera patients. And then in 1869, the lighthouse was built on top of the Southwest Bastion.

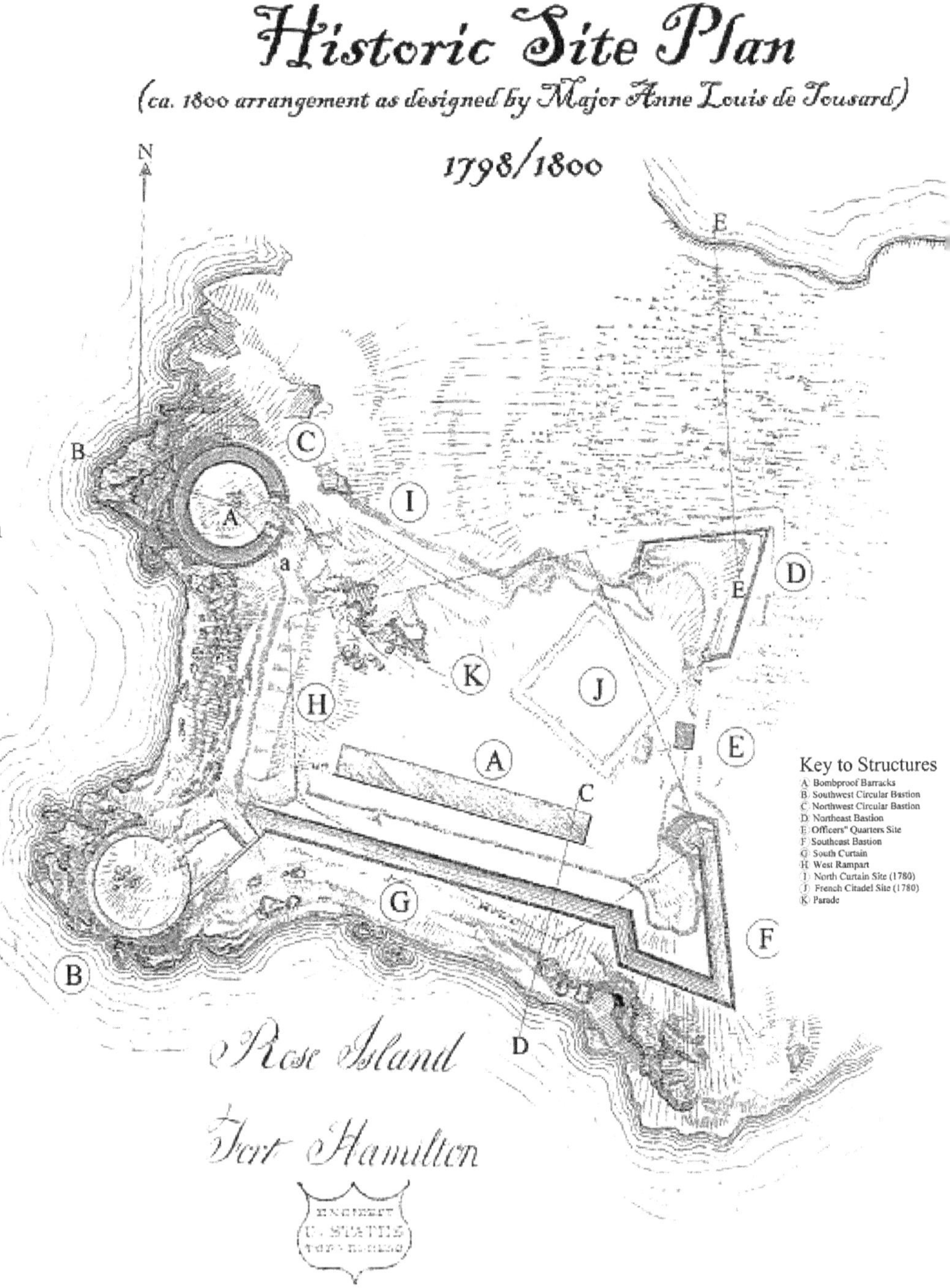

Just prior to World War I—during the time Wanton Chase lived on the island—the United States government rechristened the fort the Newport Naval Torpedo Station-Rose Island and added many new buildings: several magazines (storage for explosives and ammunition), barracks, and housing for officers.

World War II triggered more building in the 1940s, such as the construction of a torpedo warehouse, a TNT filling station, and several anti-aircraft gun emplacements to protect Narragansett Bay from invasion. The fort was abandoned in 1956 and the buildings were allowed to decay. As part of its effort to preserve history, the Rose Island Lighthouse Foundation is currently overseeing the restoration of some of the Fort Hamilton buildings.

RICHES

Five-year-old Wanton trotted after big brother Norman, their bare feet making the beach rocks crunch together like a giant grinding his teeth. The boys were in a hurry, on a mission to find treasures washed up on the beach.

"Where did you find that case of chocolate bars?" Norman asked.

Wanton pointed toward the northernmost point of the island.

"Too bad they were all wet."

Wanton shrugged. "I think they taste good salty."

"Yeah, but no one will buy them with their wrappers all wrinkled up. Let's hope we can find something else, something we can sell."

As they rounded the point and started trudging south down the far side of the island, they heard the boom of the Fort Adams sundown gun. Wanton saw something fluttering near a pile of rockweed and discovered a rectangle of what he thought was paper. But when he rinsed off the sand, he found it was a five-dollar bill, more money than he'd ever had in his whole life! "Norman, look!"

His brother trotted over. "Wow! Let's look for more."

They carefully combed the surrounding beach in the fading light of day. Finally, Norman exclaimed, "Aha!" and held up a dripping two-dollar bill.

Wanton reluctantly held out the five to his big brother.

"No, it's yours," Norman said.

"But you're older."

Norman shook his head. "Finders, keepers."

"Do you think Grandfather will let us keep the money?"

Norman shrugged. "It's not like we can give it back to anyone. But we'd better ask him."

The boys stumbled through the darkness, following the red beacon back to the lighthouse while talking excitedly about what they would purchase with their new-found money…if Grandfather let them keep it. Norman wanted a $1.98 calf-skin catcher's mitt so he could join his school's baseball team and Wanton was hoping to buy a 48-cent nickel-plated water pistol to shoot at Roger O'Connor.

They walked into the kitchen just as Grandmother was pouring the last pot of steaming water into a large oval washtub set in the middle of the wood floor. "There you two are," she said. "I was just about to send Dixie out looking for you." She nodded toward the cocker spaniel sleeping under the kitchen table. "Now get ready for your baths. I'll not have you looking like a couple of hobos in church tomorrow morning."

That night, like every Saturday night Wanton's brother and sisters were visiting, they all took a bath in the same tin tub. First the girls, from youngest to oldest—Mabel and then Christina—and then the boys—Wanton and then Norman—and then the adults—Grandmother and then

Grandfather. Mr. Fletcher, the assistant lighthouse keeper, didn't join them because he had his own wash tub in his second-floor apartment.

After Grandfather had finished bathing and was back at work, the boys slowly climbed the stairs to his desk on the landing below the lantern room. Grandfather laid down his fountain pen. "What may I do for you gentlemen?" he asked with raised bushy gray eyebrows.

Norman explained their windfall and then both boys placed their soggy money on the desk corner and anxiously awaited his decision.

Grandfather's wood chair creaked loudly as he sat back with his hands clasped together over his round belly. After a few moments of tense silence, he nodded slowly. "You each may choose one thing to buy and then use the rest of your money to start a savings account at the bank in Newport, next time you're in town."

Norman and Wanton smiled jubilantly.

Grandfather nodded and made a shooing gesture with one hand. "I suspect you'll be wanting to peruse the Sears and Roebuck Catalogue right about now, so go get to it." He picked up his pen and returned his attention to the lighthouse log.

"Yes, sir!" the boys said in unison, snatched their money off the desk, and scurried down the stairs.

TOYS

By the time the first Sears, Roebuck & Co. Catalogue came out in 1893, toys in America had already begun the transition from homemade to store-bought. Children were clamoring for the newest models and retailers were beginning to realize that the toy market was extremely profitable. An 1895 article in The New York Times stated that year's sale of dolls alone had accounted for nearly $2 million in business. Four store-bought toys popular in New England between 1910 and 1915 were squirt guns, marbles, teddy bears, and baseball gloves.

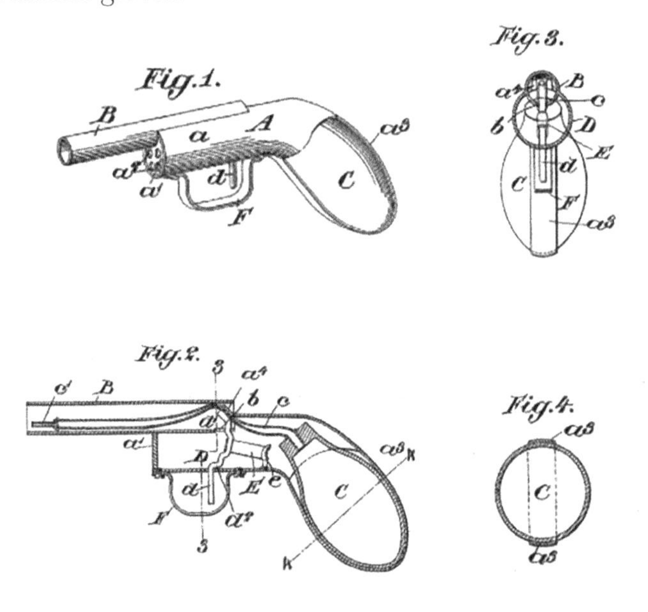

In 1896, the U.S. Patent Office issued a patent to inventor Russell Parker for the cast iron USA Automatic Liquid Pistol. The 1908 Sears catalog advertised the squirt gun by claiming it "…may be loaded or discharged as often as desired. Throws a fine stream from 10 to 20 feet and is a very practical defense against vicious dogs or tramps..." or small boys trying to conquer an island fort.

During a hunting trip in 1902, President Theodore Roosevelt refused to shoot a bear that had been tied to a tree because he felt it was "unsportsmanlike." A political cartoon about the incident appeared in the Washington Post and inspired Morris Mitchtom, a Brooklyn toy maker, to sew a tiny soft bear, which he sent to the president along with a request to market the stuffed animal as "Teddy's bear." Roosevelt agreed and a new toy was launched, which soon became one of the most popular toys in America. In their 1908 catalog, Sears, Roebuck & Co. offered models in four sizes, ranging from the 75-cents 10-inch version to the 16-inch bear for $2.38.

Martin Christensen of Akron, Ohio, patented a machine in 1903 that enabled mass-production of toy glass marbles, reducing their cost from one cent a piece to a bag of 30 for one cent, and making them affordable for most American children. The basic game of marbles was played by drawing a 3-foot circle on the ground, placing some marbles inside of it, and then trying to shoot them out of the circle, using bigger, shooter marbles. If playing "keepsies," the winner then owned all of the marbles he managed to knock out of the circle.

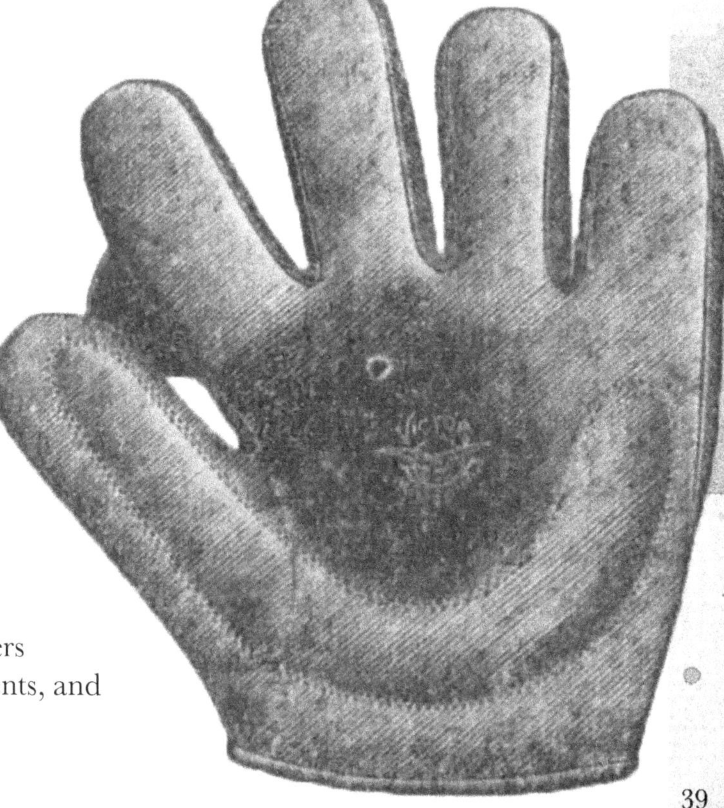

The Boston Red Sox beat the Philadelphia Phillies to win the 1915 World Series causing children all over New England to rush to join baseball teams. At that time, players could purchase a ball for 22-cents, a wooden bat for 60-cents, and a fielder's glove for $1.90.

THE OUTHOUSE

Out the lighthouse kitchen door and to the left, stood their whitewashed wooden outhouse. Wanton had been terrified of the outhouse for as long as he could remember. To him, its bench seat, with its two dark holes, looked like a perfect place for a monster to hide in wait of an unsuspecting victim. He imagined long boney fingers reaching up, grabbing him, and dragging him down, down, into a deep, dark pit.

And then there was the fact that the outhouse was perched at the very edge of the circular stone bastion upon which the lighthouse was built. In the winter, the wind whipped off the bay and roared through the tiny wood structure, making it a cold and drafty place for him to sit and do his business. Yet another reason for Wanton to dislike the outhouse.

On one chilly fall Saturday afternoon, when he was five years old, Wanton was forced to confront his outhouse fears. A few of Grandfather's friends from his days on the Newport police force had boated out to the lighthouse for a visit. Grandfather set up a table in the living room and the four of them had spent the afternoon smoking, laughing, playing poker, and drinking beer.

Wanton spent the day lying on his bed drawing pictures of birds. Late that afternoon, just as the shadows were growing long and thin, Grandfather appeared at Wanton's bedroom door. "Son, I need your help." He smelled of pipe smoke and beer. "It seems that Mr. Baldwin has dropped something he needs into the outhouse and we'll have to go down and get it for him."

Wanton recoiled with horror. "C-can't Grandmother help you?" The thought of climbing down into the monster's lair trapped his breath in his chest.

Grandfather shook his head. "She's visiting Mrs. O'Connor right now, delivering a pie, so you're going to have to hold the lantern for me," He waved his arm. "Let's go."

With a small sigh of relief at not being required to actually go into the pit, Wanton slid off his bed and stuffed his feet into his shoes. By the time he put on his jacket and got out to the outhouse, Grandfather already had put on his rubber boots, gloves, and oilskin waders; propped open the outhouse door; lifted the bench seat; and was lowering a narrow wooden ladder down into the dark hole. His friends leaned against the white fence atop the bastion wall, watching the proceedings and snickering. Wanton noticed that Mr. Baldwin's face looked funny…smaller.

Grandfather mounted the ladder and pointed his chin toward a hurricane lamp sitting on the ground outside the door. "Wanton, take that and hold it up, nice and high. Shine the light down here so I can see what's what." He began to descend, one wrung at a time.

Wanton picked up the light and shuffled his boots toward the doorway.

"Come on, boy. I haven't got all night. Get that lantern in here."

Wanton edged toward the hole. The smell was horrible.

"A little closer, boy." Grandfather's voice sounded echoey.

Wanton raised his arm up higher, swung the lamp out over the pit, and then—despite himself—he peered down, terrified of what he would see.

But all he saw was Grandfather standing ankle-deep in a very stinky, muddy-looking square hole, scooping up something with a fishing net. There were no boney fingers. No monster with fangs. In fact, there was nothing scary at all. "Got 'em," Grandfather said and climbed back up the ladder. He handed the net to Mr. Baldwin and strode down the hill toward the beach.

By the time Grandmother returned from visiting Mrs. O'Connor, Grandfather had cleaned off his boots, gloves, and waders and Mr. Baldwin had thoroughly scrubbed his dentures with strong lye soap and had popped them back into his mouth, making his face looked normal again. And Wanton was no longer afraid of the outhouse.

LIFE IN AMERICA

Like Wanton and his grandparents, in 1915 nearly 50% of American households did not have indoor toilets. Only 30% owned telephones and fewer than 20% had electric or gas-fired ranges, instead cooking their meals on wood-fired stoves like Wanton's grandmother. Very few people owned a radio or a refrigerator and clothes washers, dryers, and televisions were practically unheard of at that time. Fewer than 30% of Americans had electricity so most lit their homes with oil lanterns and heated them with fireplaces or small kerosene units in each room.

Woodrow Wilson, a former Princeton University professor and governor of New Jersey, was President of the forty-eight states of the United States, which had a population of 100 million people, fifty percent of whom were under the age of 25.

The most popular song on the radio that year was "Carry Me Back to Old Virginny" by Alma Gluck. "The Metamorphosis" by Franz Kafka was the best-selling adult book and "The Scarecrow of Oz" by L. Frank Baum topped the children's chart.

In 1915, an average single-family home cost $1,033 and a car was $941, making them both luxuries for the typical American worker, whose annual income was just $687. A loaf of bread cost 2 cents and a quart of milk was 9 cents, contributing to the fact that the price of groceries accounted for nearly 50 percent of most people's income.

In 1915, D.W. Griffith's movie, "The Birth of a Nation," was released to much protest. The film promoted racial intolerance and was credited with sparking a resurgence of membership in the Ku Klux Klan. Overseas, much of Europe was already embroiled in The Great War (World War I), but the United States remained neutral, not joining the Allies until April 1917.

TRIP TO NEWPORT

One warm spring day, just before Wanton turned six, he was being a pony, galloping through the knee-high grass near the Navy barracks, when he heard Grandfather call his name. Afraid that he'd done something wrong, he hurried back toward the lighthouse, knowing better than to make Grandfather wait.

Grandfather, with his hands stuffed into his dungaree trouser pockets, stood next to the newly-painted white rail fence that surrounded his vegetable garden. Nearly everything around the lighthouse was newly-painted white. Grandfather thought a fresh coat of whitewash made everything look "ship-shape" so he regularly painted the fences, the lighthouse, the flagpole, the oil house, the massive 10-foot high wall around the base of the lighthouse, and even the larger stone outcroppings in the yard. Sometimes Wanton worried if he stood still too long, Grandfather might try to whitewash him, too.

Pointing toward the launch moored a little way offshore, Grandfather said, "Grandmother needs to go into town, but I'm expecting a visit from the Lighthouse Service this afternoon, so I want you to go with her, help her with the skiff and the launch, and carry her parcels. Do you think you can manage that?"

Wanton nodded rapidly. He enjoyed his infrequent trips into Newport, with all of the bright colors, new sights, and bustling people to

see. And the yummy smells coming from the food stores and restaurants made his mouth water, just thinking about them.

"Good." Grandfather nodded toward the lighthouse. "Hurry and put on your church clothes. Shoes, too." Trips into Newport were pretty much the only time Wanton wore shoes in the spring, summer, or fall.

Ten minutes later, Grandmother rowed the two of them out in the skiff. And twenty minutes after that, Wanton helped her secure the launch to the pier in Newport.

"First stop is the post office," Grandmother said, but Wanton knew that already, since the post office was always their first stop when they went to town.

Holding her hand, he skipped past the horses and carts on cobblestoned Thames Street and stopped in front of the brand-new post office. Tipping back his head, he said, "Wow!" The stone and brick building, with its arched windows and carved stone medallions, was the biggest and fanciest building he'd ever seen.

"Come on then." Grandmother picked up the front of her plain black dress and stomped up the nine sharp granite steps to the entrance with Wanton close at her heels.

Inside the lobby, Wanton marveled at the rows and rows of shiny brass post office boxes and tried to step only on the black stone tiles on the floor, avoiding the white ones.

"You wait here," Grandmother said. "I'll go get our mail."

Wanton scooted back to stand beside a wall and watched a group of children following a young woman dressed in a straight dark skirt, a puffy white blouse, and a large floppy hat with a blue satin ribbon. Wanton thought she looked very pretty. As they approached him, he heard the woman say, "And now we are back at the main entrance, concluding our tour of the new post office. Does anyone have any questions about what you've seen here this morning?"

A dark-haired boy raised his hand.

"Yes, Nelson?"

"Miss Perkins, how much would it cost me to send a letter from here to my grandma in Chicago, Illinois?"

"A stamp costs two cents and if you put one on your envelope—and address it the way that Mr. Turner explained to us a few minutes ago—it can be mailed to anywhere in all 48 states of the United States."

A red-haired boy grinned. "What's the matter, Nelson? You miss your granny?"

Nelson smiled sadly. "Yes. I guess I do."

"Aww! Poor Nelson!" a bunch of the boys chorused.

But Wanton saw two girls pat the boy's back and smile kindly at him.

As the school children filed past him out the door, Nelson nodded at him and Wanton wondered what it would be like to live like Nelson: in a regular house, in Newport, with his mother and father and brothers and sisters, surrounded by a bunch of other children his age. Just for a moment, Wanton thought that sounded really nice.

NEWPORT, RHODE ISLAND

When Wanton and Grandmother stepped off the launch that April day in 1916, they entered a busy harbor town, full of bustling shops and flourishing industries. At the time, Newport was not a large city, with a population of around 25,000; nearby Providence was almost ten times bigger. But despite Newport's relatively small size, the city's populace was ethnically diverse. English, Jewish, African Americans, and Native People had formed the backbone of Newport's early colonial society. And then in the early 20th century, they had been joined by waves of immigrants from Ireland, Greece, Italy, Portugal, and various Hispanic countries, drawn to the city by work available at Fort Adams and the Naval Station.

The Navy played a vital role in Newport's history. In 1881, the Naval Recruit Training Station was established to instruct 750 young sailors annually. By 1915, the station was training thousands of recruits every year in anticipation of the U.S. entry into World War I. At that time, Wanton's father was employed as a master machinist at the Naval Torpedo Station, another Newport facility. Since its inception in 1869, the Torpedo Station was tasked with the design and testing of various forms of torpedoes and with training naval personnel in their use. Just before WWI, Rose Island's Fort Hamilton became the Naval Torpedo Station-Rose Island and was used to load and store torpedoes.

In the mid-nineteenth century's Gilded Age, Newport became the favorite place for wealthy Americans to spend their summers. Located just 75 miles from Boston and 175 miles from New York City, Newport was conveniently positioned for summer or weekend getaways. Prominent families, including the Vanderbilts, the Astors, and the Wideners, built huge "cottages" on Bellevue Avenue, affording them unrestricted views of the Atlantic Ocean. From June to August, these families took turns hosting elaborate parties and galas in their private ballrooms. Anyone who was someone was expected to attend. As keeper of the Rose Island Lighthouse, Wanton's grandfather was instrumental in guiding their yachts into Newport's harbor, but this service did not earn him an invitation to any of their parties.

Thames Street, running parallel to the waterfront, was one of the two original streets laid out in Newport in 1654. Because of its proximity to the city's wharves, it was the busiest commercial street in the city. During their visit to Thames Street, Wanton and Grandmother might have visited Koschny's First Class Confectionery; Charles Cole's Pharmacy; T. Mumford Seabury's Store, which sold "shoes for every need;" Carr's List Bookstore; Barney's Music Store; or A.C. Titus Co., offering the "best refrigerator built." In their advertisements in the Newport Mercury newspaper, many of these shops also mentioned their proximity to the new Post Office to aid prospective patrons in finding them.

DOG FIGHT

Dixie, the cocker spaniel, usually stayed close to the lighthouse, preferring Grandmother's company to all others. Most days, he could be found curled up under the kitchen table while Grandmother was preparing one of her delicious meals. Or snoozing in the yard while she hung out the laundry. Although Grandmother often complained about Dixie being "constantly under foot," she seemed to genuinely enjoy the dog's company.

When Dixie did wander off the lighthouse lawn, he often would get into scuffles with Gunner O'Connor's Labrador, Blackie. Being much smaller and gentler than the O'Connor's dog, Dixie usually suffered major injuries in these encounters.

In June, a few weeks after Wanton turned seven, he heard the dogs growling and barking at each other and went running toward the O'Connor's house. By the time he got to their yard, both of Dixie's ears were bleeding, he had a big gash on one of his rear legs, and Blackie's jaws were clamped around his throat, pinning the cocker spaniel to the grass. Roger O'Connor stood a short distance away, with his hands tucked under his armpits, laughing.

Wanton ran to rescue Dixie, only to be repelled by a snarl and a low growl from Blackie. "Call him off!" he pleaded with Roger.

The older boy shrugged. "Why should I? Your stupid dog came into our yard. He's getting what he deserves."

Once again, Wanton tried to help Dixie and once again he was warned off by Blackie's teeth. The cocker spaniel now yipped in pain. "Please make him stop!"

Roger laughed harder.

Fortunately, just then Mrs. O'Connor stepped out the side door. "Roger, get Blackie off of their dog this instant!" she said.

Roger obeyed.

Wanton knelt near Dixie to survey the damage. He counted no fewer than six open wounds, including a nasty bite on the dog's front paw that prevented him from walking. Despite Wanton's small size, he scooped up his family's pet and trudged toward the lighthouse.

Mrs. O'Connor called after him, "Please tell your grandmother we are sorry and we hope your dog isn't hurt too badly."

Wanton staggered into the lighthouse kitchen and stood in the middle of the floor holding the bleeding dog, his arms and legs shaking from the strain of carrying him halfway across Rose Island. Grandmother swiped everything off the kitchen table. "Put him up here," she said. "I'll go get my sewing kit."

With Wanton's help, Grandmother cleaned and dressed all of Dixie's wounds, putting a few stitches in the larger gashes to hold them closed. When they were done and the dog was resting comfortably under the table, Wanton and Grandmother collapsed onto the living room sofa. She hugged him and kissed the top of his head. "It's a good thing you were here to help me with Dixie, Wanton. I don't know what I'm going to do when you move back home this fall to go to school."

Wanton hugged her back and wished that day would never come.

EDUCATION IN AMERICA

Although seven-year-old Wanton wished he could remain on Rose Island and forgo attending public school, he had no choice. In the late 1800s, American educational reformer John Dewey had introduced the concept of progressive education, promoting the idea that all children should be taught academics to encourage them to reach their full potentials. This philosophy was adopted nationally and quickly changed the nature of education in America. In 1900, 31 states mandated school attendance for children aged 8 to 14, but by 1915, just five years later, it was required by all 48 states, resulting in a seventy-two percent enrollment rate.

Schools in Newport, Rhode Island, were typical of most New England towns. Younger children attended neighborhood elementary and middle schools and then, if they were permitted by their families, they went to the large, town-wide Roger's High School. At that time, the "high school" movement was still in its infancy and the graduation rate among youths in New England was only 16%. This rate was partially due to the stringent requirements imposed upon high school students. In 1915, a student at Roger's was required to pass both an oral and a written exam in every subject every year to progress to the next grade and then had to pass a comprehensive exam at the end of his senior year to graduate.

In 1915, most Newport teachers were women. In fact, seventy-five percent of teachers nationwide at that time were women, who were hired with strict limitations placed upon their behavior. For example, that year the Cabell County West Virginia Board of Education mandated that its women teachers were not allowed to marry, could not dress in bright colors, and under no circumstances may they loiter in downtown ice cream parlors. Many teachers, especially those in rural areas, were expected to live in their students' homes, rotating from one home to another every month or so. Their pay was very low and their freedoms were greatly restricted, since teachers were expected to instruct their students on academics in the classroom and on morals and ethics through personal example.

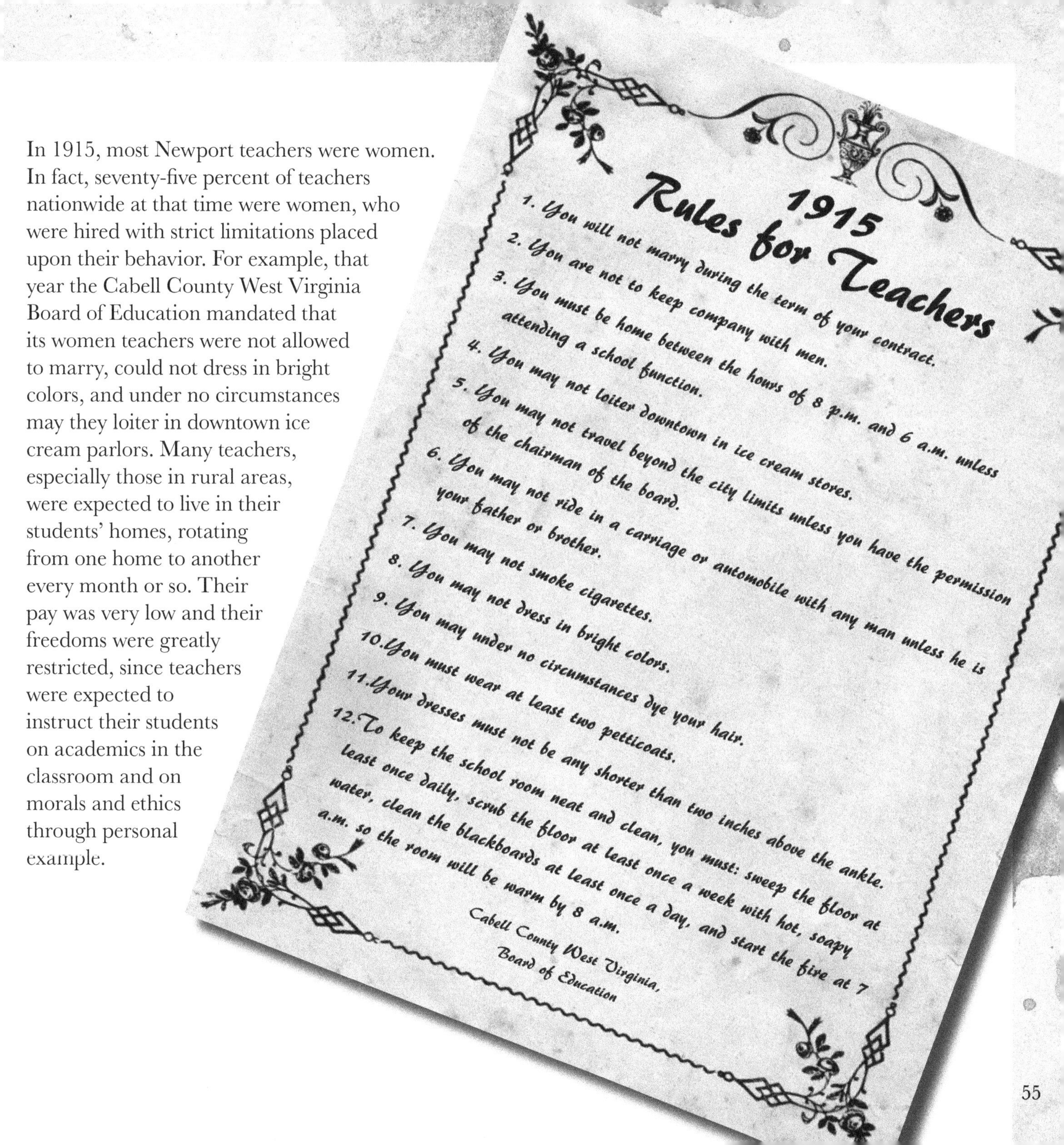

1915
Rules for Teachers

1. You will not marry during the term of your contract.
2. You are not to keep company with men.
3. You must be home between the hours of 8 p.m. and 6 a.m. unless attending a school function.
4. You may not loiter downtown in ice cream stores.
5. You may not travel beyond the city limits unless you have the permission of the chairman of the board.
6. You may not ride in a carriage or automobile with any man unless he is your father or brother.
7. You may not smoke cigarettes.
8. You may not dress in bright colors.
9. You may under no circumstances dye your hair.
10. You must wear at least two petticoats.
11. Your dresses must not be any shorter than two inches above the ankle.
12. To keep the school room neat and clean, you must: sweep the floor at least once daily, scrub the floor at least once a week with hot, soapy water, clean the blackboards at least once a day, and start the fire at 7 a.m. so the room will be warm by 8 a.m.

Cabell County West Virginia,
Board of Education

LEAVING ROSE ISLAND

Seven-year-old Wanton sat alone in the dark on the bench near the south wall of the lighthouse bastion, tears dripping from his chin onto his dirty blue cotton shirt. He'd spent the day finishing his fort, digging it out of the hill in the center of the island, and his clothes showed evidence of his strenuous efforts. But the fort was finally done, complete with a small American flag proudly raised on a wooden pole, planted directly in the fort's center. Of course, he had no choice but to finish the fort that day, sincc tomorrow he was leaving Rose Island.

Another tear plopped onto his chest as he stared out at the lights of all the huge ships currently in and around Newport Harbor. To his right, gigantic battleships were anchored along the Jamestown shore. Some of the sailors from the USS Pennsylvania had visited the lighthouse last week, laughing and joking with Wanton and calling him their little brother. And then on his left, near Newport, the cruisers and destroyers were anchored. One after the other, lights glittered from boats moored in a line for as far as he could see. Some of those sailors had come to Rose Island, too, climbing to the top of the lighthouse tower on their day off. And Wanton had enjoyed their visits. He'd liked showing them around the lighthouse and around the island, sharing his home with them.

But starting tomorrow, this would no longer be his home. In the morning, he was due to move back in with his mother, father, brother, and two sisters to their house on Ledyard Place in Newport, a house he hadn't live in for nearly six years now. The house, the neighborhood, the town, and—to a large extent—his immediate family were all strange to Wanton. The lighthouse, Rose Island, Grandmother, Grandfather, and Dixie were what he considered his home and family. And he didn't want to leave them.

But school started in Newport in a few days and by law Wanton was required to attend. He'd also overheard his mother talking to Grandmother, saying, "It will be good for Wanton to move back home. He's been too isolated out at the lighthouse for far too long."

But Wanton liked his isolation. It was the only life he'd ever known. What was he going to talk about with other children? How would he get along with them? The only other kid he'd played with besides his brother and sisters had been Roger O'Connor and that hadn't gone very well; they usually ended up getting into fights or throwing things at each other. What was he going to do with a whole classful of children?

"Wanton, time to come in for bed," Grandmother called from the lighthouse.

He obediently rose and returned to the kitchen. Closing the door behind him, he stared out through its four panes of glass at the lights across the bay, tears continuing to making dark spots on his blue shirt.

"What is the matter, Wanton?" Grandmother asked.

"I don't want to leave here and live in Newport!" he replied and then ran to his bedroom.

* * *

After a brief adjustment period, Wanton Chase went on to live a very happy and productive life on the "mainland." He graduated from Newport's Roger's High School and became a machinist, toolmaker, and planner for the Navy's Newport Torpedo Station. In his spare time, he enjoyed playing tennis and ice hockey and crewing for sailing regattas. He married, had two children, and lived with his family in Newport for 66 years, until moving to a nearby retirement community, where he remained until his death at the age of 99.

* * *

As an adult, Wanton wrote, "When I think of my days on Rose Island I don't remember being cold in the winter or lonesome. I always found something to do on the beaches. Unlike these days of programs and supervision and toys for young people I provided my own fun for the day." Wanton often said that he was grateful for his time at the lighthouse and that it had made him a very self-reliant person. "I never get bored with myself."

AMERICA ENTERS THE GREAT WAR

The Great War, later known as World War I, began on July 28, 1914, when Austria-Hungry declared war on Serbia. The war quickly escalated and eventually involved Austria-Hungary, Germany, Bulgaria, and the Ottoman Empire (the Central Powers) fighting Great Britain, France, Russia, Italy, Romania, Japan, and the United States (the Allied Powers). At its beginning, most Americans favored a policy of isolationism and President Woodrow Wilson pledged that the United States would remain neutral. But at the time, Great Britain was one of America's major trading partners. So, when German mines caused disruption of trade by damaging and even sinking commercial vessels bound to and from Great Britain, tensions between the United States and Germany grew. And then when German ships actually torpedoed and sank several American vessels, U.S. sentiment turned against Germany and the Central Powers. The May 1916 sinking of the British ship, Lusitania, which killed 1,200 of the 2,000 passengers aboard, convinced many Americans that isolationism was no longer the correct policy to follow.

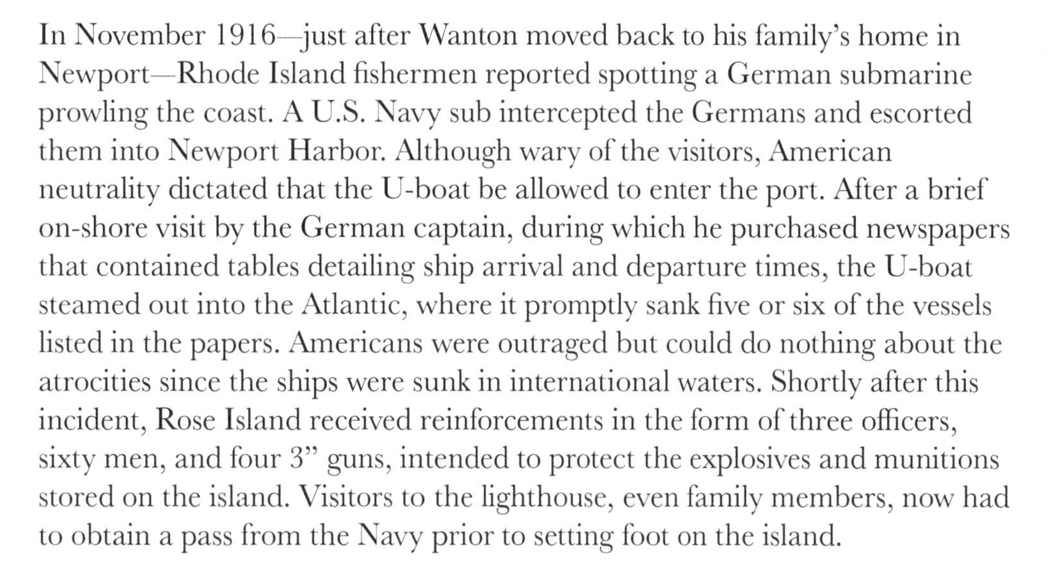

In November 1916—just after Wanton moved back to his family's home in Newport—Rhode Island fishermen reported spotting a German submarine prowling the coast. A U.S. Navy sub intercepted the Germans and escorted them into Newport Harbor. Although wary of the visitors, American neutrality dictated that the U-boat be allowed to enter the port. After a brief on-shore visit by the German captain, during which he purchased newspapers that contained tables detailing ship arrival and departure times, the U-boat steamed out into the Atlantic, where it promptly sank five or six of the vessels listed in the papers. Americans were outraged but could do nothing about the atrocities since the ships were sunk in international waters. Shortly after this incident, Rose Island received reinforcements in the form of three officers, sixty men, and four 3" guns, intended to protect the explosives and munitions stored on the island. Visitors to the lighthouse, even family members, now had to obtain a pass from the Navy prior to setting foot on the island.

Early in 1917, Congress passed a bill providing funding to prepare America to enter the war. And then on April 6, after four more U.S. merchant ships were sunk by German U-boats, the United States formally declared war and joined the Allied Powers. In late June, the first U.S. soldiers arrived in France and by November 1918, a year and a half later, the "war to end all wars" was over.

By the end of the war, Wanton's grandfather was no longer keeper of the Rose Island Lighthouse. In 1918, the U.S. Congress passed a law mandating retirement for any employees of the Lighthouse Service over the age of 70, so in July of that year, 78-year-old Captain Charles Curtis was replaced as lighthouse keeper. He and Christina moved in with Wanton and his family in Newport and lived there until their deaths in 1922.

ROSE ISLAND LIGHTHOUSE FOUNDATION

In July 1984, Rhode Islanders from various environmental and neighborhood groups joined together to form the Rose Island Lighthouse Foundation, which was authorized by the City of Newport to restore and maintain the lighthouse and its surrounding grounds as a public historic site. The property was approved for nomination to the National Register of Historic Places, the city officially obtained the deed to the island, and restoration of the lighthouse began.

Originally the Foundation planned to restore the lighthouse to its appearance when it was decommissioned in the 1970s, but when they received historical photographs showing the lighthouse in the 1920s, they decided to restore it to that era instead. The badly decayed exterior was stripped to the frame and rebuilt with white clapboard siding, colorful slate roof shingles, and decorative door and window trim.

The building's interior was also gutted and then furnished with new wiring, plumbing, and a radiant-floor heating system. The walls were plastered, a new septic field was installed, and a cistern was built to provide water for cooking and cleaning. In all, the renovation cost over a million dollars, generously provided through grants and donations. In 1992, the Rose Island Lighthouse was opened to the public and then on August 7, 1993, its beacon was relit to once again flash its light across Narragansett Bay every evening.

The first floor of the restored lighthouse is a museum, open daily from Memorial Day to Labor Day, which accurately depicts life as a lighthouse keeper in 1920. The second floor of the building serves as quarters for guests, who rent out the lighthouse and serve as its keepers for a week at a time, choosing to work from one to eight hours a day. Two rooms on the first floor and several more in the nearby restored barracks building are available for guests to rent for shorter terms.

A wildlife refuge, meeting spaces, and picnic areas are available for groups and events and guided tours are offered throughout the summer months. Access to the lighthouse and Rose Island is provided via the Jamestown/Newport Ferry.

The Lighthouse Foundation staff and volunteers also do important work with school groups, delivering environmental and historic information about Rose Island. Over 900 students visit the island on field trips every year. In total, the island welcomes more than 3,000 visitors annually: day-trippers, guest lighthouse keepers, students, and those who attend special events there.

If you would like to learn more about the Rose Island Lighthouse or would like to make a much-appreciated donation to the Lighthouse Foundation, please visit their website: www.roseisland.org. Donations support on-going restoration of the lighthouse and other buildings, education and research development, and upkeep of the facilities and grounds.

THE BOOK TEAM

Lynne Heinzmann (author) also wrote the historical novel Frozen Voices (New Rivers Press, 2016), winner of the Fairfield Book Prize. She is a wife, mother, friend, author, architect, stained-glass artist, and beagle-lover who lives in North Kingstown, Rhode Island. For more information about Lynne and her writing, please visit www.LynneHeinzmann.com.

Julia Heinzmann (illustrator) is an early childhood art educator in Boston. A graduate of the University of Rhode Island with degrees in both art and education, Julia enjoys drawing pictures, boating, and playing with cats.

Michaela Fournier (graphic designer) has a passion for all things creative. She challenges herself with DIY projects and enjoys spending time with family and friends. Born and raised in Rhode Island, Michaela loves the unique history that makes the state so exceptional.

Marilyn Harris (researcher) is a retired enrichment teacher, but these days you might find her in colonial garb telling stories to visitors at Smith's Castle, a 340-year-old museum house in North Kingstown, RI. Her history obsessions are eclectic though. At various times she has been an ancient Egyptian, the "Unsinkable Molly Brown" (who was never called Molly), and an accused witch in Salem. She is truly a woman of many faces and talents.

CPSIA information can be obtained
at www.ICGtesting.com
Printed in the USA
LVHW071143240220
647909LV00026B/931